the STORY of JONAH

Retold by JULIANA BRAGG • Illustrated by CHARLES E. MARTIN

GOLDEN PRESS • New York
WESTERN PUBLISHING COMPANY, Inc. • Racine, Wisconsin

Long, long ago there was a man named Jonah who lived a good life and always obeyed God's laws. He thought of himself as a true man of God.

One day God spoke to Jonah.

"Jonah," he said, "there is a city called Nineveh far away. It is filled with wicked people who live wicked lives. Go there and tell those people that I am going to destroy them and their city."

Jonah didn't want to go to Nineveh. "It is too far away," he said to himself. "Those people don't even know about God. Anyway, they will never believe what I tell them. They will laugh at me, or chase me out of the city. They might even try to hurt me, or kill me."

The more Jonah thought about those wicked people, the more frightened he became. He decided to run away.

That very night he packed a few things and hurried to the seaport.

There he found a ship that was getting ready to sail far across the sea.

"Please let me come with you," he begged the captain. "I'll give you all my money for a place on your ship."

The captain was glad to take Jonah's money.

Jonah hurried on board the ship and hid deep in the hold. At last he heard the noise of the anchor being drawn up onto the deck. Then he felt the sway of the ship as it headed out into the open sea.

Jonah sighed with relief. He would make a new life for himself. God would never find him now.

But nobody can hide from God.
When the ship was far out from land, God sent
a terrible storm. Black clouds filled the sky.

A great wind blew over the sea, whipping the waters
into huge waves that beat against the sides of the ship.
"We're sinking!" cried the captain. "Lighten the ship!
Throw the cargo overboard!"

Some of the sailors ran down into the hold to get the cargo. There they found Jonah, sleeping soundly with a smile on his face.

"Wake up! Wake up! We're sinking!" they shouted. "We must get the cargo off the ship!"

Up on deck it was as dark as night. The wind roared and the ship tossed wildly. The sailors began to throw the cargo overboard.

Suddenly Jonah realized that only one thing would save the ship. "You must throw me overboard," he shouted to the captain. "God has sent this storm to punish me. I tried to run away from him and now he has found me."

No one wanted to throw Jonah into the sea to drown. But the wind and the waves were too much for them.

Finally the sailors grabbed Jonah and threw him into the sea. At once the wind stopped and the sea became calm.

Down, down, down into the
sea sank Jonah. He was drowning.
    But God was not yet finished with Jonah.
He sent a great fish swimming through the
deep to swallow him up in one gulp.

Jonah woke up in the stomach of the great fish. It was dark. He could hardly see. But he could hear the beating of the fish's heart and the gurgling of its stomach. He could feel the swaying of its body as it swam in the sea.

Jonah was glad that God had saved him from drowning. But he was afraid, too.

And God listened to Jonah. He wanted to give him another chance. So God made the fish spit Jonah out onto the land. And Jonah thanked God for saving him.

Then God spoke to Jonah again.
"Jonah, I want you to go to Nineveh and
tell the people what I told you to tell them."

"People of Nineveh!" Jonah called out as he walked through the streets and marketplaces. "The Lord God says he will destroy you and your city because of your wicked ways!"

The people did not laugh at Jonah or try to hurt him. They believed him. They went home and took off their fancy clothes and dressed in simple rags. They stopped stuffing themselves with fine food and rich wines. They began to pray, asking God to forgive them.

Even the king of Nineveh took off his royal robes as a sign of sorrow for all the wicked things he and his people had done.

When Jonah had finished his work, he climbed a hill outside the city and sat down to watch God destroy Nineveh.

But God was pleased that the Ninevites had listened to Jonah. He decided to give them another chance.

Now Jonah was angry. "I knew this would happen," he complained. "My work is wasted and I feel like a fool."

"Jonah, Jonah," said God gently. "Will you never learn what I am like? My love is great. It is greater than my anger. And it is for all my creatures. Didn't I give you another chance?"

Jonah nodded.

"So have I given the Ninevites another chance. Go now, Jonah, and try to love as I do. Then you will be a true man of God."

So Jonah began his long journey home, and tried to live his life as God had taught him.